Robin Hood

Little John

WALT DISNEY PRODUCTIONS
presents

Robin Hood

and the Great Coach Robbery

RANDOM HOUSE NEW YORK

Library of Congress Cataloging in Publication Data
Disney (Walt) Productions.
Robin Hood and the great coach robbery.
(Disney's wonderful world of reading, #15)
Disguised as fortune tellers, Robin Hood and Little John stop Prince John's coach, tell
his fortune, and carry off his gold.
[1. Robin Hood—Fiction. 2. Adventure stories] I. Title. PZ7.D625Ro [E] 73-18738
ISBN 0-394-82554-3 ISBN 0-394-92554-8 (lib.bdg.)
Manufactured in the United States of America
I J K   3 4 5 6

Long ago there was a bad prince
called Prince John.

He lived in a castle.

He had lots and lots of gold.

Prince John loved his gold.

He even slept with it.

But Prince John wanted more gold.

He sent for the Sheriff.

"The poor people still have a little gold left," he said. "Take it!"

The poor people had to give their last gold coins to the Sheriff.

Then they had no money to buy food.

But the poor people had two friends called
Robin Hood and Little John.
They lived in the forest.
Robin and Little John did not like the prince.
They knew he took money from poor people.

Robin and Little John thought
of a way to help the poor people.
They sneaked into the castle
when Prince John was sleeping.
They sneaked out of the castle
with some of his gold.

Then they gave it back to the poor people.
Everyone was happy again.

But Prince John was not happy.
He was so angry he hopped
up and down on his throne.
He said to the Sheriff:
"Bandits are stealing my gold.
Catch them!"

The Sheriff and his men chased
the bandits into the forest.

But Robin and Little John knew the forest
better than the Sheriff did.
And so they got away.

One day Robin and Little John were
hiding in some bushes.

Suddenly they saw the royal coach
going through the forest.

"It is Prince John!" said Little John.

"He must be taking his gold for a ride," said Robin.

They ran to their trunk of old clothes.
Robin gave Little John a dress.
"Quick! Put this on," said Robin.
"We can pretend we are fortune tellers."
"Why can't we just be bandits?"
asked Little John.

They got dressed as they raced
through the forest.

Little John put on an orange dress
and a yellow wig.

Robin put on a blue dress
and a black wig.

At last they came to the royal coach.

The royal elephants were pulling it.
The royal rhinos were carrying
the royal box of gold.

Inside the coach sat the bad prince and his servant, Sir Hiss.

The prince was playing with his bags of gold.

"Hiss, do you know what it means when I rob the poor?" said Prince John.

"What does it mean, Sire?" said Hiss.

"It means I get very rich," said the prince.

"You are also very handsome," said Hiss.
"Look at yourself in this mirror."

"What a face!" cried Prince John.
"And to think it is all mine."

Just then Prince John heard someone calling
to him.

"Yoo-hoo, Prince! Would you like to have
your fortune told?"

Prince John and Sir Hiss peeked out.

"Fortune tellers!" cried Prince John.

"They might be bandits," said Hiss.

"Bandits—in dresses?" said the prince.

"You must be joking. Stop the coach."

"Your Royal Highness," said Robin.
"We can do strange and wonderful things.
May we tell the royal fortune?"

"Of course, you may," said Prince John.

"You may even kiss the royal hands."

Robin kissed the prince's left hand.

As he kissed it, he took off the royal ring.

Sir Hiss saw him do it.

"Sire," hissed Hiss. "He took . . ."

"AACK!" cried Prince John.

"Stop hissing in my ear, Hiss. It tickles."

Then it was Little John's turn
to kiss the prince's right hand.
    As he did so, the royal jewels
disappeared.

Little John grinned.
    There — between his teeth —
were the royal jewels.
    Sir Hiss saw them.

"Sire," hissed Hiss.
"He has . . ."

"ARGGH!" cried the princ
"This hissing in my ear
has got to stop."

Prince John grabbed Hiss by the throat.
"You have hissed your last hiss, Hiss,"
said Prince John.

He tied a knot in Sir Hiss's throat and
stuffed him in a basket.

"You worry too much, Hiss," said Prince John.
"You are giving the royal head
a royal headache."

Robin went into the coach.
"Now close your eyes, Sire,"
said Robin. "I will call the spirits."
"Oh, my! Spirits!" said Prince John.
And he closed his eyes.
"Yoo-hoo, Spirits!" called Robin.

Little John was outside.

He had a balloon on a stick.

The balloon was filled with fireflies.

When Robin called to the spirits,

Little John put the balloon into the coach.

"Aha!" cried Robin. "The spirits come
in a strange and wonderful ball."

Prince John opened his eyes.

"That looks like a balloon to me," he said.

"Hush," said Robin. "I see a face inside
the ball."

"Is it my face?" asked Prince John.

'It is a royal face," said Robin.

"A kind face . . .

a handsome face . . .

a wise face."

'Then it must be mine," said Prince John.

As Robin told the prince's fortune,
he took the bags of gold.

"You have a great fortune!" said Robin.

"Oh, I knew it would be good," said the prince.

Robin dropped the bags of gold out the door.

Little John was busy, too.

He was taking the gold hub caps off the wheels.

Nearby the royal rhinos were taking a nap.
Between them sat the royal box of gold.
Little John drilled a hole in the box.
The royal rhinos went right on snoring.
ZZZZZZZZZZZZZZZZ.

After he drilled the hole, the gold fell out.
Little John caught it in a big bag.
CLINKETY–CLINKETY.
The royal rhinos went right on snoring.
ZZZZZZZZZZZZZZZ.

Just then Robin jumped out of the coach.
He was wearing the royal robe.

Little John and Robin ran off into the forest.

Prince John opened his eyes.

He saw that the fortune teller was gone.

Then he saw that everything was gone.

His jewels, his gold, his royal robe!

All he had on was his royal underwear.

He threw open the curtains and yelled:

"I have been robbed! After them, you fools!"

His yells scared the royal elephants.

They began to run with the coach.

But there were no hub caps to hold
the wheels on.

So the wheels came off.

The coach went crashing down to the ground.
Prince John and Sir Hiss went flying
out the door.

They landed in the mud with a royal splat.
"I hate to be an I-told-you-so," said Hiss,
"but I told you so."

When he got back to the castle,
Prince John sent for the Sheriff.

"Who are these bandits?" he asked.

"Their names are Robin Hood and
Little John," said the Sheriff.
"They are friends of the poor people."

"From now on they are outlaws,"
said Prince John.

Once more Robin and Little John gave
the gold to the poor people.

Then they went back to the forest.

"Are we really outlaws?" asked Little John.

"We are outlaws as long as Prince John is the prince," said Robin. "But someday we will be heroes. You wait and see."

Prince John

The Sheriff

Sir Hiss